A Christmas Tree for Ruby

Grosset & Dunlap
An Imprint of Penguin Group (USA) Inc.

Based upon the animated series *Max & Ruby*
A Nelvana Limited production © 2002–2003.

Max & Ruby™ and © Rosemary Wells. Licensed by Nelvana Limited NELVANA™ Nelvana Limited. CORUS™ Corus Entertainment Inc. All Rights Reserved. Used under license by Penguin Young Readers Group. Published in 2012 by Grosset & Dunlap, a division of Penguin Young Readers Group, 345 Hudson Street, New York, New York 10014. GROSSET & DUNLAP is a trademark of Penguin Group (USA) Inc. Manufactured in China.

ISBN 978-0-448-46231-8   10 9 8 7 6 5 4 3 2 1

ALWAYS LEARNING   **PEARSON**

It was almost Christmastime.
Grandma was taking Max and Ruby to
Santa's Tree Land.
"We need to find the perfect tree!" said Ruby.

"It shouldn't be too tall, too short, or too skinny."
"It should be just right!" said Grandma.

But Max wanted to visit Santa.

"You can't visit Santa right now, Max," said Ruby. "We have to get our tree first or they'll all be gone."

"We'll go see Santa just as soon as we find our tree, Max," said Grandma.

"Okay," said Max.

Grandma, Ruby, and Max walked around and looked at trees.

"How about this one, Ruby?" asked Grandma.

"It is nice and bushy," said Ruby, "but it's too small."

"How about this one, Ruby?" asked Grandma. "It's nice and tall!"

"I like that tree," said Ruby, "but it's crooked. The ornaments will fall off."

"You're right, Ruby," said Grandma. "Let's keep looking."

"How about this one?" asked Grandma.

"It's not too tall and not too short. It's perfect!" said Ruby.

"Max, what do you think?" said Grandma.

But Max was gone.

Ruby found Max waiting to see Santa.

"Santa!" said Max.

"You can't visit Santa yet, Max. Come see the perfect tree we found!"

But when they went back to the tree, it was gone.
"Oh no!" said Ruby. "Somebody took our tree!"
"That's okay, Ruby," said Grandma. "We'll find another one, just as perfect!"

Grandma, Ruby, and Max looked for another tree.

"I like this one!" said Ruby. "Max, what do you think?"

But Max was gone again.

Ruby found Max on Louise's sled.
"Where are you going, Max?" said Ruby.
"Santa Claus!" said Max.
"Max, not yet. Come see my perfect tree!"

But when Ruby and Max returned to the tree, it was gone.
Somebody had taken Ruby's perfect tree again!

19

"Don't worry, Ruby," said Grandma. "We'll find another tree."

"Okay, Grandma," said Ruby. "How about this one? It's a little too skinny, a little too short, and a little too crooked, but I still like it," said Ruby.

"It is nice," said Grandma. "Max, what do you think?"

But Max was gone again.

Grandma and Ruby found Max sitting on Santa's lap.

"There you are, Max!" said Grandma.
"What did you ask Santa for?" said Ruby.

"Christmas tree!" said Max.